פסח

פסח

פסח

פסח

פסח

פסח

פסח

פסח

פסח

פסח

פסח

פסח

פסח

פסח

פסח

פסח

פסח

פסח

פסח

פסח

פסח

פסח

פסח

פסח

פסח

פסח

פסח

פסח

פסח

פסח

פסח

פסח

פסח

פסח

פסח

פסח

פסח

פסח

פסח

פסח

פסח פסח פסח פסח פסח

פסח פסח פסח פסח

פסח פסח פסח פסח פסח

פסח פסח פסח פסח

פסח פסח פסח פסח פסח

פסח פסח פסח פסח

פסח פסח פסח פסח

פסח פסח פסח פסח פסח

A First Passover

by Leslie Swartz

Illustrated by
Jacqueline Chwast

SIMON & SCHUSTER BOOKS FOR YOUNG READERS
Published by Simon & Schuster
New York   London   Toronto   Sydney   Tokyo   Singapore

SIMON & SCHUSTER BOOKS FOR YOUNG READERS
Simon & Schuster Building, Rockefeller Center, 1230 Avenue of the Americas, New York, New York 10020
Copyright © 1992 by The Children's Museum, Boston. First SIMON & SCHUSTER BOOKS FOR YOUNG READERS edition 1994. Originally
published by Modern Curriculum Press as part of the Multicultural Celebrations series created under the auspices of The
Children's Museum, Boston. Leslie Swartz, Director of Teacher Services, organized and directed this project with funding from
The Hitachi Foundation. All rights reserved including the right of reproduction in whole or in part in any form. Many thanks to
Sophie Schiller for contributing her family stories. Designed by Gary Fujiwara. Photographs: 14, Blair Seitz; 17, Bill Aron; 20,
Catherine Ursillo. SIMON & SCHUSTER BOOKS FOR YOUNG READERS is a trademark of Simon & Schuster. Manufactured in Mexico.
10 9 8 7 6 5 4 3 2 1   ISBN 0-671-88025-X

▲▲▲▲▲▲
The
Children's
●●●●●●
Museum
●●●●●
Boston

Winters in Moscow were cold and dark. In the afternoons, I would race home to my grandfather who was waiting in our apartment. Every afternoon my grandfather sat in the kitchen, sipping his hot tea from a small glass.

First he would listen to me tell about my day at school.

Then, as the wind roared and the snow piled up outside, Grandfather would smile and tell me stories about when he was growing up. "Our house was always full of aunts and uncles and cousins and lots of happy talk."

But Grandfather would frown when he told about what happened when he became a young man. "It was a terrible time," he said. "Many people were put in prison for no reason. Jews had to be especially careful. It was not good to be a Jew in the Soviet Union."

2

When the first signs of spring began to appear and the trees were budding, my grandfather always told me my favorite story from Jewish history. It was the *Passover* story. It went like this:

Over 3,000 years ago, the Jews were slaves in Egypt. A shepherd named Moses went to ask Pharaoh, the ruler of Egypt, to let the Jews leave Egypt and be free. Each time Pharaoh said no. After each 'no,' the people of Egypt were struck with a terrible plague. But each plague passed over the Jews and did not harm them.

The last plague was the most horrible of all. Finally, Pharaoh said the Jews could go free. Moses led them quickly out of Egypt on foot. They left so quickly that there was not time to let their bread dough rise before they baked it. So when they took it out of the oven, it was flat like a cracker, and they called it matzoh.

And always, when he ended the story, Grandfather would give me a big bear hug. He would always remind me, "Jasha, you're never too old for a hug from your *Zayde*."

I never told anyone outside of my family this *Passover* story. It was a secret. "Jews have to be careful in the Soviet Union," my parents always said.

"Jasha, someday we will leave the Soviet Union," my mother told me. "Jews have a hard life here. It will be hard for you to go to the university if we stay. Life is too uncertain and there is no hope that things will get better."

"We will go to live with your Uncle Daniel in America," my father said, waving the letter from his brother that he kept in his desk drawer.

"When will we leave?" I asked my mother.

Her answer was always the same. "When we get permission . . . who knows when that will be."

One night an old friend of my grandfather appeared at our door. Did we want to order any *matzoh*? It was another secret. There was no place that Jews could buy *matzoh* in Moscow. Grandfather's friend promised to make it and bring it to us in time for *Passover*.

"Nathan, we will buy your *matzoh*, but please bring it at night," my father told him. "We do not want anyone to know we are celebrating *Passover*."

The next week we took the train to Uncle Sam's and Aunt Anna's house in the country. It was a long ride, but I loved getting out of the city. We brought Nathan's *matzoh* wrapped in newspaper. At Uncle Sam's and Aunt Anna's house, we drew the shades and ate the *matzoh* with dinner.

At dinner, Grandfather told my favorite story again. Everyone listened carefully. I knew that all Jews, no matter where they live, tell this story at *Passover*. At the end of the story, Grandfather whispered to me, "Someday, we too will go free—like the Jews in Egypt," and he gave me a big bear hug.

I wondered if he was as wise in this as he was in other things.

I got my answer more quickly than I expected.
About two weeks later, my father came home early.
He was bursting with news.

"I have it! I have it!" he said, waving a postcard he
had just received. "We have gotten permission to
leave. We are going to America where my brother
Daniel lives. But we must be ready quickly."

We packed what we could in a short time. We
didn't even have a chance to say goodbye to
friends. We were going to a new country. But
unlike the Jews in Grandfather's story, we took a jet
plane to freedom—to America.

At first everything in our new country was strange and different. School was noisy. Everyone spoke English so quickly. And the food wasn't the same . . . the white bread was tasteless!

Here in America, after regular school, I go to Hebrew school where I am learning what it means to be a Jew. I am learning to read Hebrew and the *Torah*.

Now when Grandfather waits for me in the afternoons, I have exciting things to tell him. "Would you believe, Grandfather, that all your stories are in the *Torah*?" But Grandfather does not seem at all surprised.

14

Tonight we will celebrate our first *Passover* in America. It will be different. This year there will be no *matzoh* man coming to our door. We can buy all the special *Passover* foods at the supermarket. My mother says we will have a *Passover* feast with wonderful *gefilte fish* and chicken soup with *knaidlech*.

Tonight we will go to my Uncle Daniel's house for the *Seder*. We won't have to draw the shades. We will read from the *Haggadah* and we will learn about all the special foods that are symbols of *Passover*—the *karpas*, *matzoh*, *maror*, *haroset*, roasted lamb bone, roasted egg, and cups of wine.

Tonight I will ask in Hebrew, "Why is this night different from all other nights?"

Now I know the answer to that question. Tonight is the night to celebrate freedom for all Jews, and all people, whether they are in Egypt, the Soviet Union, or anywhere.

But tonight there is one thing that will not be different. My grandfather will once again tell the story of *Passover*, and give me a big bear hug. And this time we all know that this story is my family's story, too.

Glossary

(Some of these words are *Hebrew* and some are *Yiddish*, two of the languages spoken by Jewish people.)

gefilte fish (geh-FILL-teh FISH) a Yiddish word for chopped fish cakes cooked with onion, egg, and seasoning, and served cold

Haggadah (hahg-GAH-dah) a book telling the Passover story and used to conduct the Seder

haroset (hahr-OH-set) a Hebrew word for a mixture of apples, nuts, and wine; it is a symbol of the mortar used by Jewish slaves to build Egyptian cities

karpas (KAHR-pahs) a Hebrew word for green herbs, such as parsley; it is a symbol of springtime and new life

knaidlech (K'NAYD-lahch) a Yiddish word for "matzoh balls;" Passover dumplings

maror (mahr-OR) a Hebrew word for bitter herbs, such as horseradish; it is a symbol of the bitterness of slavery

matzoh (MAHT-soh) unleavened bread; traditionally eaten for the eight days of Passover

Passover (PAHS-oh-vur) a Jewish holiday in memory of the freeing of the ancient Hebrew people from slavery in Egypt

Seder (SAY-dur) a ceremonial feast observed on the first and sometimes the second night of Passover

Torah (toh-RAH) a sacred handwritten parchment scroll on which is written the Five Books of Moses in Hebrew; it contains Jewish literature and tradition

Zayde (ZAY-deh) a Yiddish word for grandfather

About the Author

Leslie Swartz is the Director of Teacher Services and China Specialist at The Children's Museum, Boston. A former history teacher, Ms. Swartz has created kits, curriculum materials, and videotapes on cultural topics. She was raised in a Jewish family; her father and grandparents came from the Soviet Union. *A First Passover* is based on Sophie Schiller's family's story.

About the Illustrator

Jacqueline Chwast was born, raised, and attended art schools in Newark, New Jersey. She has illustrated newspapers, magazines, and books for many years. Ms. Chwast currently teaches a course called "Concepts in Illustration" at the Parsons School of Design in New York City.

פסח   פסח   פסח   פסח   פסח

פסח   פסח   פסח   פסח

פסח   פסח   פסח   פסח   פסח

פסח   פסח   פסח   פסח

פסח   פסח   פסח   פסח   פסח

פסח   פסח   פסח   פסח

פסח   פסח   פסח   פסח   פסח

פסח   פסח   פסח   פסח

פסח   פסח   פסח   פסח   פסח